SPONGEBOB DETECTIVEPANTS

The Case of the Missing Spatula

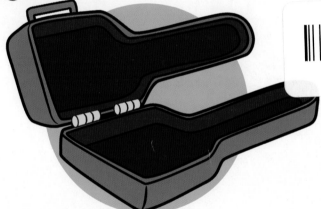

by David Lewman   illustrated by Harry Moore

Based on the TV series *SpongeBob SquarePants*® created by Stephen Hillenburg as seen on Nickelodeon®

SIMON SPOTLIGHT/NICKELODEON

An imprint of Simon & Schuster Children's Publishing Division · New York London Toronto Sydney · 1230 Avenue of the Americas, New York, New York 10020

Copyright © 2006 Viacom International Inc. All rights reserved. NICKELODEON, *SpongeBob SquarePants*, and all related titles, logos, and characters are registered trademarks of Viacom International Inc. Created by Stephen Hillenburg. All rights reserved, including the right of reproduction in whole or in part in any form. SIMON SPOTLIGHT and colophon are registered trademarks of Simon & Schuster, Inc. Manufactured in China

6 8 10 9 7 5
ISBN-13: 978-1-4169-1319-1   ISBN-10: 1-4169-1319-X

"Good morning, Mr. Krabs!" SpongeBob said cheerily.

"Arrggh," answered Mr. Krabs, fumbling with the front door lock. "Ready to fry up a lot of Krabby Patties today, SpongeBob?"

"Today and every day, sir!" SpongeBob shouted. "I'm ready! And so is Flipper!" He held up his carrying case.

"Ah, your favorite spatula," Mr. Krabs said, opening the front door. "That

Then SpongeBob spotted Squidward. "Good morning, fellow Krusty Krab employee!" SpongeBob called, waving happily.

"What's so good about it?" Squidward mumbled.

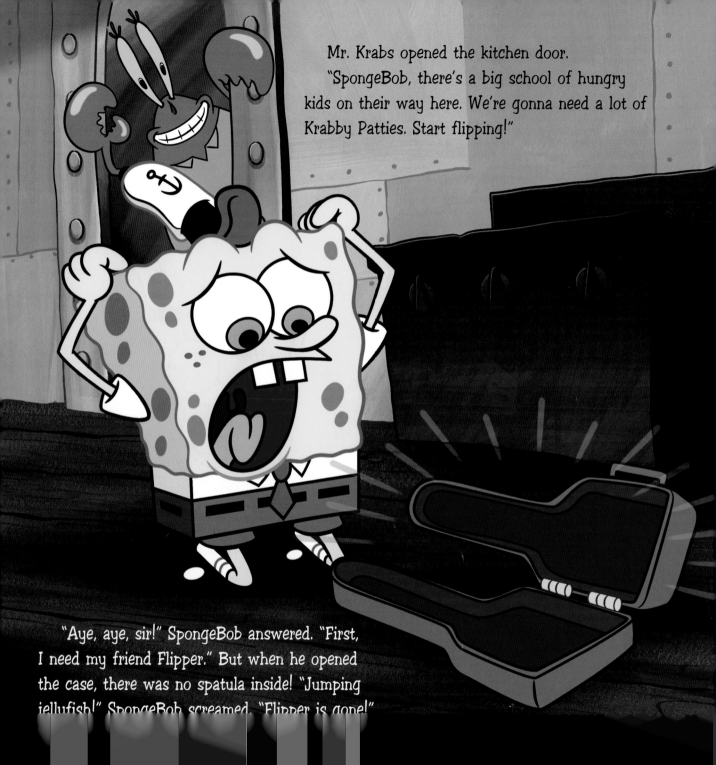

Mr. Krabs opened the kitchen door. "SpongeBob, there's a big school of hungry kids on their way here. We're gonna need a lot of Krabby Patties. Start flipping!"

"Aye, aye, sir!" SpongeBob answered. "First, I need my friend Flipper." But when he opened the case, there was no spatula inside! "Jumping jellufish!" SpongeBob screamed. "Flipper is gone!"

"Flipper is my favorite spatula," cried SpongeBob. "I can't fry without him!"

Just then Patrick came in. "Hey, SpongeBob!" he called. "I've been waiting for you at Goo Lagoon! We're gonna make sand castles, remember?"

"Patrick, my spatula is missing!"

"Oh, no!" cried Patrick. "You can't work without your spectacles!"

"Spatula," corrected Squidward.

"That's missing too?" Patrick asked with surprise.

"We'll have to be detectives. Let's question the witnesses."

"Mr. Tentacles," SpongeBob said. "What do you know about the case of the missing spatula?"

"Nothing," said Squidward.

"And you, Mr. Krabs?" asked SpongeBob. "What can you tell us about Flipper's disappearance?"

"Flipper is missing!" shouted Mr. Krabs. "Without Flipper, there are no Krabby Patties, which means no customers and no money!"

"Calm down, Mr. Krabs. We're on the case!" SpongeBob said. He turned to Patrick.

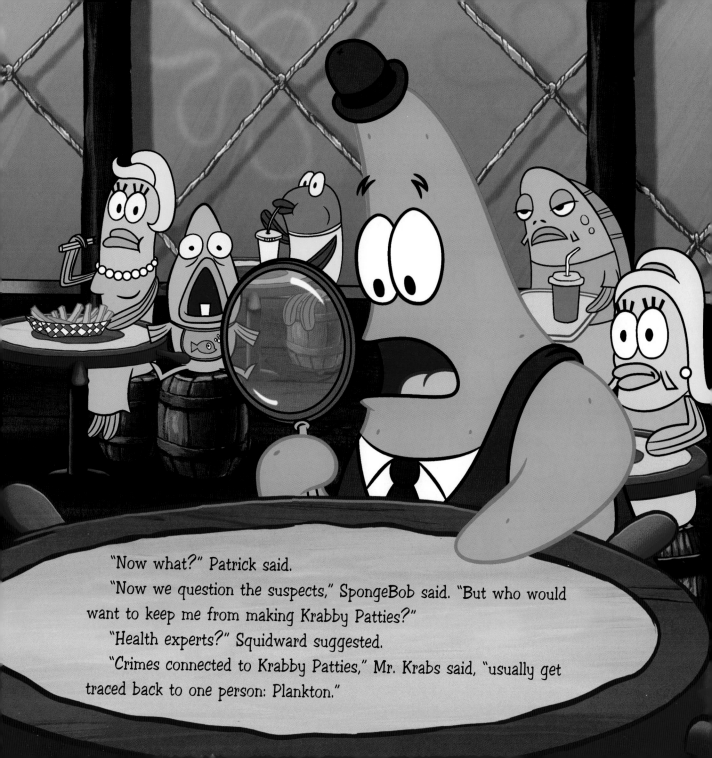

"Now what?" Patrick said.

"Now we question the suspects," SpongeBob said. "But who would want to keep me from making Krabby Patties?"

"Health experts?" Squidward suggested.

"Crimes connected to Krabby Patties," Mr. Krabs said, "usually get traced back to one person: Plankton."

The door of the Chum Bucket burst open. Plankton jumped to his feet. "Hot dog!" he yelled. "Customers!"

"Not customers," SpongeBob said. "Detectives!"

"Give back SpongeBob's spectacles!" Patrick shouted accusingly.

"Um, spatula, Patrick," said SpongeBob gently.

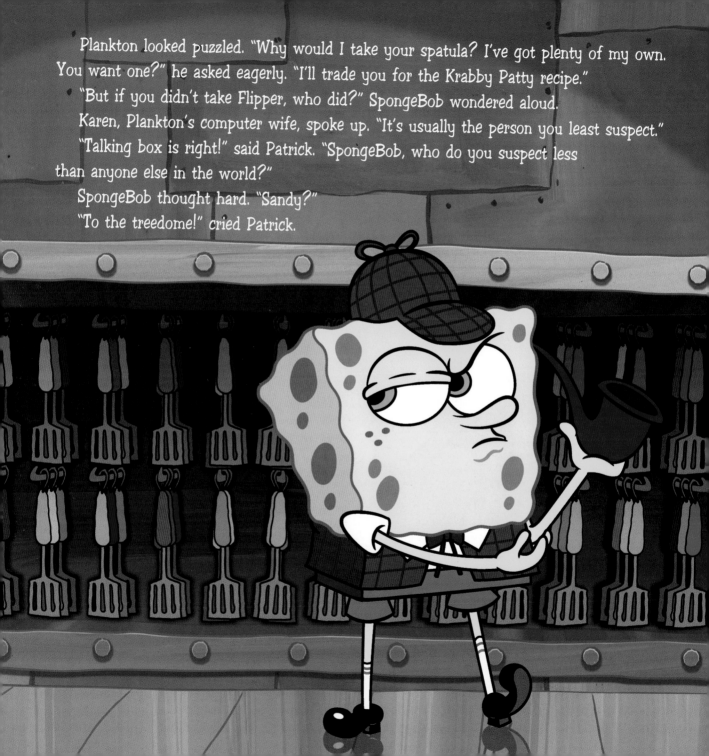

Plankton looked puzzled. "Why would I take your spatula? I've got plenty of my own. You want one?" he asked eagerly. "I'll trade you for the Krabby Patty recipe."

"But if you didn't take Flipper, who did?" SpongeBob wondered aloud.

Karen, Plankton's computer wife, spoke up. "It's usually the person you least suspect."

"Talking box is right!" said Patrick. "SpongeBob, who do you suspect less than anyone else in the world?"

SpongeBob thought hard. "Sandy?"

"To the treedome!" cried Patrick.

"You lost your favorite spatula?" Sandy asked. "That's terrible, SpongeBob!"
"You haven't seen it, have you, Sandy?" SpongeBob asked hopefully.
Sandy shook her head. "I sure haven't. You haven't seen it at all today?"

"Nope," answered SpongeBob sadly. "Oh, Flipper, where are you?"

Patrick searched through Sandy's yard with his magnifying glass, but he didn't find anything except a couple of worms.

"Well," asked Sandy, "where were you yesterday?"

SpongeBob thought for a minute. "Driving school," he said.

"Then maybe you left your spatula there!" Sandy said.

Mrs. Puff sighed. "No, SpongeBob, I haven't seen your spatula. Think, SpongeBob," she said patiently. "Where did you last see your spatula?"

"At my house," he said. "I sleep with it. It helps me dream of Krabby Patties."

"Then you should go home and check there," suggested Mrs. Puff.

"Thanks, Mrs. Puff!" shouted SpongeBob as he dashed out of the classroom.

Patrick and SpongeBob ran to his pineapple.

"I put Flipper in his case and laid it right on this trunk," SpongeBob said.

"A-ha!" said Patrick. "There are smudges on this trunk!"

SpongeBob tasted one of the smudges. "Mmm . . . chocolate! Like the ice cream we ate last night!" SpongeBob said.

"Footprints!" Patrick cried. "Round footprints!"

"Let's follow them!" said SpongeBob. "Being a detective is so exciting!"

SpongeBob and Patrick followed the footprints all the way to Goo Lagoon. "Oh, boy!" Patrick said. "The beach! We can build sand castles!"

"Patrick, we're looking for my spatula, remember?" Suddenly SpongeBob spotted a familiar handle sticking out of the sand. "Flipper!" SpongeBob cried as he pulled out his beloved spatula. "Flipper! What are you doing here?"

"That's not Flipper, that's my digger," Patrick said, confused. "I'm using it to make sand castles. I borrowed it from your house last night after we ate that chocolate ice cream."

SpongeBob hugged his favorite spatula. "Patrick, you're the one who took Flipper!"

"Wow," said Patrick. "Talking box was right. It always is the one you least suspect!"

Back at the Krusty Krab, Mr. Krabs stuck his head in the door of the kitchen. "Ready for all those customers, SpongeBob?"

"I'M READY!" shouted SpongeBob. "And so is Flipper!" That day SpongeBob made the best batch of Krabby Patties he'd ever made!

SpongeBob SquarePants
LIGHTS, CAMERA, PANTS!

SPONGEBOB GOES MULTIPLAYER!

www.SpongeBobthevideogame.com

© 2005 THQ Inc. © 2005 Viacom International Inc. All Rights Reserved. Nickelodeon, SpongeBob SquarePants and all related titles, logos, and characters are trademarks of Viacom International Inc. "SpongeBob SquarePants created by Stephen Hillenburg. Exclusively published by THQ Inc. THQ and the THQ logo are trademarks and/or registered trademarks of THQ Inc. All rights reserved. "PlayStation" and the "PS" Family logo are registered trademarks of Sony Computer Entertainment Inc. TM, ®, Game Boy Advance and the Nintendo GameCube logo are trademarks of Nintendo. Microsoft, Xbox and the Xbox logos are either registered trademarks or trademarks of Microsoft Corporation in the U.S. and/or other countries and are used under license from Microsoft.

EVERYONE
E
Cartoon Violence
CONTENT RATED BY ESRB

www.nick.com
www.thq.com

NICK
SpongeBob SquarePants

SpongeBob SquarePants is excited to start another glorious day at his wonderful job, frying Krabby Patties at the Krusty Krab. But when SpongeBob discovers that his favorite spatula, Flipper, is missing, he resolves never to fry again until he finds out who stole it! Will SpongeBob ever make Krabby Patties again? Have fun with the holographic stickers while SpongeBob solves this mystery!

by David Lewman   illustrated by Harry Moore

Look for more books about SpongeBob SquarePants at your favorite store!

SIMON SPOTLIGHT/NICKELODEON
Simon & Schuster, New York
Nontoxic
Manufactured in China
VISIT OUR WEB SITES: www.SimonSaysKids.com and www.nick.com

created by
Stephen Hillenburg

Look for
SpongeBob SquarePants
books in Spanish!

US $5.99 / $6.99 CAN
ISBN-13: 978-1-4169-1319-1
ISBN-10:   1-4169-1319-X
EAN
9 781416 913191
0706

T3-BYO-242